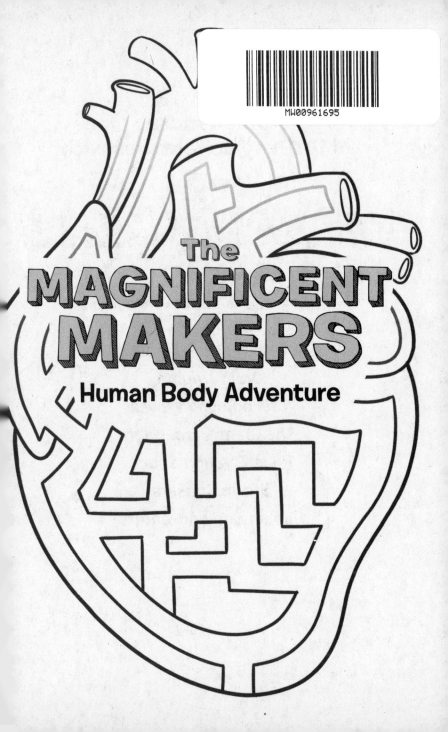

The

MAGNIFICENT
MAKERS

Human Body Adventure

Go on more
a-MAZE-ing adventures with

The
MAGNIFICENT
MAKERS

The MAGNIFICENT MAKERS 7

Human Body Adventure

by Theanne Griffith
illustrated by Leo Trinidad

A STEPPING STONE BOOK™
Random House 🏠 New York

Text copyright © 2023 by Theanne Griffith
Cover art copyright © 2023 by Reginald Brown
Interior art by Leo Trinidad, inspired by the work of Reginald Brown

Visit us on the Web!
rhcbooks.com

Educators and librarians, for a variety of teaching tools, visit us at
RHTeachersLibrarians.com

Library of Congress Cataloging-in-Publication Data
Names: Griffith, Theanne, author. | Trinidad, Leo, illustrator.
Title: Human body adventure / by Theanne Griffith; illustrated by Leo Trinidad.
Description: First edition. | New York: Random House Children's Books, [2023] |
Series: The magnificent makers; 7 | "A Stepping Stone book." |
Audience: Ages 7–10. | Summary: When best friends Pablo and Violet return to the Maker Maze to learn about the human body with their third-grade classmate Lorenzo, they also realize how teasing can lead to hurt feelings.
Identifiers: LCCN 2022012852 (print) | LCCN 2022012853 (ebook) |
ISBN 978-0-593-56310-6 (paperback) | ISBN 978-0-593-56311-3 (library binding) |
ISBN 978-0-593-56312-0 (ebook)
Subjects: CYAC: Human body—Fiction. | Makerspaces—Fiction. | Teasing—Fiction. |
LCGFT: Novels.
Classification: LCC PZ7.1.G7527 Hu 2023 (print) | LCC PZ7.1.G7527 (ebook) |
DDC [Fic]—dc23

Printed in the United States of America
10 9 8 7 6 5 4 3 2 1

First Edition

This book has been officially leveled by using
the F&P Text Level Gradient™ Leveling System.

Random House Children's Books supports the
First Amendment and celebrates the right to read.

In memory of the courageous
Christopher "Deuce" Wheeler II
—T.G.

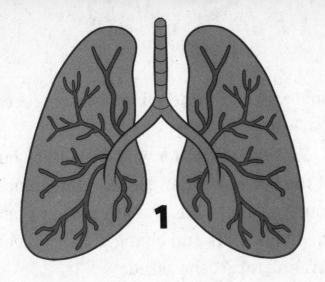

Best friends Pablo and Violet rode their bikes through the crisp morning air toward Newburg Elementary.

"That's impossible!" Violet yelled over her shoulder.

Pablo stood up to pedal his silver-and-black bike. "I'm serious! Inside our bodies, blood is blue," he called.

"Then why is it red *outside* our bodies?" she asked.

"Well . . . ," Pablo began. "I'm not sure.

But I watched a video about it last night on YouTube."

Violet giggled. Her wild curls stuck out of the bottom of her helmet. "Blue blood sounds super fake, Pablo." She gripped the handlebars and changed the subject. "Wanna race?" she asked.

Pablo nodded and shouted, "Last one to school is a rotten cucumber!"

Pablo and Violet had been best friends since they were six years old when Pablo moved to Newburg from Puerto Rico. Even though he was still learning English, they quickly found they liked doing the same things. Like playing soccer during recess and eating pickles at lunch. They also disliked the same things, like cucumbers. But what really made them best friends was how much they both *loved* science. Pablo wanted to become an astronaut and explore space. And ever since Violet could remember, she'd wanted to be a scientist who helped others by finding cures for all kinds of diseases.

"Better hurry! You're starting to turn cucumber green!" Violet teased. Her long legs sent her wheels spinning as she zoomed ahead.

Pablo pumped his legs with all his

might. His heart raced as fast as the pedals on his bike. Suddenly, he realized they were almost to the end of the bike path.

"Slow down, Violet! You win!" he yelled.

But Violet was too far ahead to hear him.

"I'm gonna win! I'm gonna win!" she yelled into the air. Violet looked down at the dashed white line on the pavement. She was going so fast it looked solid! Violet grinned as she lifted her eyes. *Haha,* she thought. *He'll never catch me now.*

"Aaaaaaaah!" someone hollered a few feet in front of her.

"Aaaaaaaah!" Violet replied with a yelp of her own. She swerved around the screaming student. Her bike screeched to a halt.

"Are you okay?" she asked, hopping down. "I didn't see you walking there, Lorenzo."

"No wonder you didn't see him," Pablo grumbled as he pulled up and parked his bike. "You were going way too fast *and* looking at the ground!"

"No I wasn't," Violet replied. "I was just going faster than you." She stuck her tongue out jokingly.

Lorenzo was still frozen in place. His eyes bounced back and forth between Violet and Pablo.

"You're okay, right?" Violet asked her stunned classmate.

Lorenzo snapped out of it and nodded. "Yeah, I'm fine. That was a close one. And I definitely don't need any more injuries. Not with the regional championship coming up." He raised his arm, which was in a neon orange cast dotted with notes from family and friends.

"How did you do that?" asked Pablo.

"Did it hurt?" added Violet.

Lorenzo tucked some loose strands of light brown hair behind his ears. "Wrestling. And yes, it hurt pretty bad. I was about to pin the girl I was competing against. But she flipped me at the last second, and I landed funny."

Brrrring! Brrrring!

Pablo folded his arms. "That's the warning bell. We should head inside. Mr. Eng doesn't like it when we're late."

Violet sighed and shook her head. "We're not going to be late, Pablo. We have five minutes, and our classroom is, like, thirty seconds away. You're always in such a rush."

"You can be late if you want to, but I'm heading inside. Plus, I'm excited for our science unit," Pablo said.

"What are we learning about? I don't remember," said Lorenzo.

"The human body," Pablo replied. "*And* I heard that Mr. Eng has a surprise for us."

"Ohhh, sounds cool! Let's go!" said Lorenzo, heading toward the school's main entrance.

Violet took her helmet off and began to lock up her bike. "Maybe Dr. Crisp will have a surprise of her own," she whispered to Pablo.

Pablo's worried face softened into a smile. "Maybe . . . ," he said as the two best friends made their way to class.

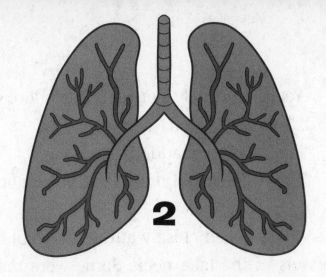

2

The students of Mr. Eng's third-grade class were seated and waiting for the school day to begin. The room buzzed with whispers about the model of a human body sitting on Mr. Eng's desk. It had tan skin that covered its face. But they could see the organs inside its chest and the muscles on its arms!

"I want muscles like those!" Lorenzo exclaimed. "Is that thing real?"

"Can't be," replied Pablo.

"Yeah, definitely not real. But it looks so . . ." Violet paused.

"Real," Lorenzo added.

"Look!" Pablo pointed. "I told you blood could be blue."

Violet looked closely at the fake blood vessels in the fake neck. Some were red and some were blue. She bit her lip as her hand shot into the air.

"Mr. Eng!" she said in a hurried voice.

"Yes, Violet?"

"Blood isn't blue, right?"

"No, blood isn't actually blue," answered Mr. Eng.

"*HA HA!* I told you, Pablo," said Violet as she crossed her arms and leaned back in her chair.

"Violet, it's not nice to tease," Mr. Eng reminded her.

"Especially not your *best* friend," Pablo said under his breath.

Violet shifted in her chair before mumbling, "Sorry, Pablo."

"It's okay," Pablo mumbled back.

Violet raised her hand again. "Since blood *isn't* blue . . . why are *those* blood vessels blue?"

"Scientists and doctors use blue and red colors to show which blood vessels *bring* blood to the heart and which *send* blood out of the heart," Mr. Eng explained.

This time Pablo raised his hand. "Veins are blood vessels that bring blood back to the heart, right?"

"That is correct," Mr. Eng replied.

Pablo turned to Violet and smiled with his chin in the air.

"Hmph," Violet grumbled.

"And arteries send blood out to the body." Mr. Eng picked up a pencil and began to trace the model blood vessels. *"AR-ter-ees,"* he repeated. "Oxygen makes our blood bright red," he continued. "And blood leaving the heart has a lot of oxygen, thanks to our lungs. That's why arteries are colored red. When the blood gets back to the heart, it has very little oxygen. That makes it darker. Veins are colored blue to show this difference." Then he passed around worksheets to everyone in the class.

Introducing Organ Systems

In the human body, a system is a group of organs that work together for a specific purpose. Here are three examples:

Digestive system
(die-JEST-iv)
- Breaks down food for the body to use as energy
- Organs: esophagus (e-SOF-uh-gus), stomach, and the small and large intestines

Circulatory system
(SUR-cue-la-tor-ee)
- Moves blood through the body
- Organ: heart
- Includes blood and many kinds of blood vessels

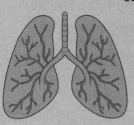

Respiratory system
(RES-per-a-tor-ee)
- Allows us to breathe
- Sends oxygen to blood
- Includes the trachea (TRAY-kee-uh, also called the windpipe), bronchi (BRON-kye), lungs, and diaphragm (DIE-a-fram)

"Whoa," said Lorenzo, looking over his sheet. He dug a finger under his cast to scratch his arm. "The human body is *complicated*."

"Especially the respiratory system. *TRAY-kee-uh. BRON-kye,*" Pablo said slowly. "Who made these words up?"

"It's not *that* bad," replied Violet.

"Yeah, well, maybe for you it's not." Pablo folded his arms and frowned. "But these words are tough for me."

"It takes practice, Pablo," Violet replied.

"My coach always says practice makes perfect!" added Lorenzo.

"Yeah, just don't ask YouTube for help. You might find a video that says we can breathe through our eyes or something." Violet giggled.

"That's not funny, Violet." Pablo huffed and turned away from his friend.

"Pablo . . . it was just a joke!" Violet shook her head and raised her hand again. "Mr. Eng, what does it mean when we say something goes down the wrong pipe? Does it go down our windpipe?"

"Actually, yes," Mr. Eng replied. "Our esophagus and trachea start out as one tube. Then they split. The trachea goes to your lungs, and the esophagus goes to your stomach. When food or water slips down your trachea, we say it went down the wrong pipe."

Mr. Eng bent over behind his desk and grabbed a large plastic bag. "You're all asking really good questions," he continued. "I think these will help answer them." He pulled out a cloth doll and pulled a zipper down its center. The inside had various organs. Just like the larger model! Mr. Eng tossed a doll to each student. Curious whispers filled the classroom.

Violet caught her doll and hurried to unzip it. When she did, her eyes popped with excitement. Sticking out from between the doll's two lungs was a small card.

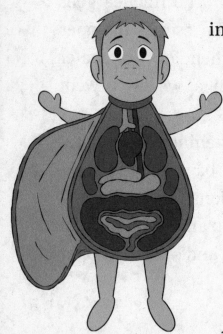

"Pablo!" Violet said in a hushed voice.

Pablo pretended he didn't hear her. He was still upset that she had made fun of him in front of the class—and for watching too much YouTube!

"Hey!" she said a little louder.

Pablo finally glanced over and saw the card. Then he couldn't help but smile. "I knew it." He leaned over to read the riddle with Violet.

ROSES ARE RED, AND BLOOD IS, TOO.
THE _____ SYSTEM SENDS
IT EVERYWHERE!
(AND NO, BLOOD ISN'T BLUE.)

BUT WHAT MAKES BLOOD RED?
IS IT SOMETHING IN THE AIR?
OXYGEN! AND THE _____ SYSTEM
MAKES SURE WE HAVE PLENTY TO SPARE!

FEELING A LITTLE SLUGGISH?
JUST HAVE A SNACK!
YOUR _____ SYSTEM BREAKS
DOWN FOOD TO GIVE YOU
YOUR ENERGY BACK!

SOLVE THIS RIDDLE TO ENTER
THE MAKER MAZE.

"Dr. Crisp must want you to know blood isn't blue, too." Violet giggled.

Pablo's frown returned.

"Oh, Pablo, I'm just messing with you," Violet said with a smile.

"Well, you're being more mean than funny. Let's just solve the riddle."

Violet cleared her throat. "Anyway, the first one is the circulatory system."

"I'm pretty sure the next one is the respiratory system," Pablo replied. "We breathe in oxygen."

"This riddle was super easy!" said Violet. "The last one is the digestive system."

The two best friends held tight as everything in the room began to tremble and shake. Dolls bounced on tables, and the model human body crashed to the floor. Organs flew everywhere! But

Violet and Pablo weren't worried. They were ready.

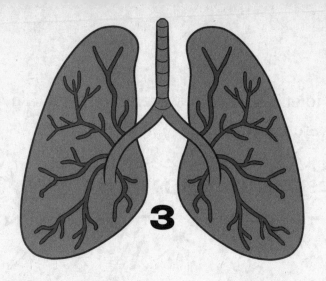

The trembling stopped and everything was still. This happened each time the portal to the Maker Maze opened. Now Violet and Pablo just had to find the ring of purple light that would actually send them to the Maker Maze.

"What's going on?" squeaked a voice.

Violet and Pablo turned to see who it was. Lorenzo was looking around the room at his frozen friends. His hands were gripping the table so tightly his knuckles had turned white.

"Yay! You're coming with us!" said Violet.

"Where?" asked Lorenzo with a confused face.

"The Maker Maze!" Violet and Pablo responded.

Lorenzo looked like he wanted to ask another question. Before he could, Violet said, "You'll see when we get there."

"But first, we need to find the portal," added Pablo. He saw a purple light out of the corner of his eye. "This way!" he shouted.

The friends hurried over behind Mr. Eng's desk. Their teacher was frozen in front of the class with his finger in the air.

"Excuse me, Mr. Eng," Violet joked.

Lying on the floor was the model human body. Glowing around it was a ring of purple light.

"Cool! Are we in a video game or something?" asked Lorenzo.

Violet and Pablo laughed. "The Maker Maze is better than *any* game out there," replied Pablo. He put his three middle fingers down and said, "Maker's honor."

"Cool. I still don't get what the Maker Maze is, but it sounds like fun!" Lorenzo exclaimed. Then he bent over to get a better look at the ring of light. "So how exactly do we—" Lorenzo didn't finish his sentence.

BIZZAP!

He was sucked into the portal! Pablo and Violet jumped in after him.

BIZZAP!

The Makers fell through the darkness for a few seconds before landing on the floor of the Maker Maze.

"Ahhh, feels good to be back!" said Violet, stretching her hands over her head.

"You weren't kidding. This *is* better than a video game!" said Lorenzo.

Violet and Pablo gave Lorenzo a quick tour while they waited for Dr. Crisp to show up. They led him down the long lab tables that housed strange plants, creepy bugs, and flasks filled with colorful bubbling liquids. Pablo pointed out his favorite gadget. Then Violet showed Lorenzo the large microscope. That was her favorite piece of lab equipment.

"We go through one of those doors to start the challenge," explained Pablo. He peered down a long hallway lined with doors.

Lorenzo squinted. The hallway was so long he couldn't see where it ended. "Whoa, that's a lot of doors."

"Each challenge has three levels," added Violet. "We need to finish the challenge in one hundred twenty Maker Minutes. That's when they unfreeze," she said, showing Lorenzo a screen above them. Their classmates back in Newburg Elementary were still frozen in place.

"If we don't finish in time, we can't come back to the Maker Maze," said Pablo.

Lorenzo smiled. "I love a good challenge! Just like wrestling. Game on!" he cheered with fists in the air.

"We need to find Dr. Crisp first," Violet began. "She runs this place."

"And goes with us on the challenge," added Pablo.

"What's shakin', Makers?" hollered a voice from behind.

It was Dr. Crisp! She removed some stained gloves from her hands and tossed them onto the floor. She had a black oil smudge on her face.

"Sorry I'm late!" said Dr. Crisp. "One of the robots got sick, so I was doing some repairs. Hey there, Lorenzo! Cool cast!"

"I broke my arm wrestling," he replied slowly. He gazed up at the rainbow-haired scientist in purple pants standing in front of him. "Wait," he said. "How do you know my name?"

Dr. Crisp reached for a backpack on one of the long lab tables. She pulled out the glittery golden Maker Manual.

"This gal knows it all!" she replied. "And she tells me everything." Dr. Crisp winked. "So, Makers. What are you in the mood to learn today?" She opened the book to a page with a giant question mark on it.

"The human body!" Violet and Pablo shouted.

The pages began to turn with increasing speed. They flipped faster and faster until they came to a very sudden stop on a page that read:

LEVEL 1:
GO WITH
THE FLOW

Enter through
door number
eight.

Dr. Crisp snapped the book shut and tossed it into her backpack. She knelt to look Violet, Pablo, and Lorenzo in the eye. "Who's with me?"

"We are!" the Makers replied.

"Thumpin' thermometers! That's what I like to hear!" Dr. Crisp turned and stomped with high knees down the never-ending hallway.

As the Makers followed, their Magnificent Maker Watches appeared on their wrists.

"Oh cool! What's this?" asked Lorenzo.

"I'll explain in a second. We should go!" said Pablo.

The Makers chased after Dr. Crisp until arriving at door number eight. Their watches glowed and vibrated as they entered. The challenge had begun.

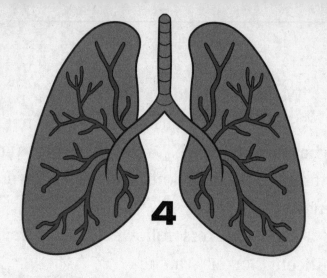

4

The room behind door number eight was bright and white. In the center was a long lab table. The Makers walked over and stood next to it.

Lorenzo couldn't stop staring at his watch. "Can we take these home?" he asked Dr. Crisp.

"I'm afraid not," she replied. "Maker Maze rules. But you will have fun with them today!"

"Yeah! They can shoot lasers and blast out holograms!" explained Violet.

"Lasers!" Lorenzo repeated.

"Yup! And they help us stay on time," added Pablo.

"Remember, Pablo *really* doesn't like to be late," Violet said to Lorenzo while she nudged Pablo with her elbow.

"I just want to be able to come back to the Maker Maze," Pablo snapped. He crossed his arms.

"I'm sure you will!" Dr. Crisp added. "If we can get started." She smiled and wiggled her eyebrows. Then she turned to Lorenzo. "Here's another cool thing these watches can do." She pressed a button on the side of her watch and shouted, "Maker Maze, activate Heather the Heart!"

BOOM! SNAP! WHIZ! ZAP!

A blast of purple fog filled the room. The Makers fanned it away from their faces. A few moments later it started to clear. Four large objects were now lying on the lab table. Two were blue and two were red.

"Okay, Makers. Listen up!" yelled Dr. Crisp with a clap of her hands. "For this first level, you must solve two different problems." She held two fingers in the air.

"First, you'll need to put Heather the Heart together correctly. Then you'll have to figure out which way blood flows through the heart."

"Yes! I love puzzles!" said Lorenzo. "It's like when I'm on the mat and need to figure out my plan of attack." He squatted into a wrestling position.

Dr. Crisp laughed. "Nice moves, champ!"

Pablo looked at the lab table and scratched his cheek. "Dr. Crisp, how are we supposed to put these pieces together? They look kind of . . . heavy."

"You're right, Pablo. I forgot to mention one little thing." Then she pressed another button on her watch.

BIZZAP!

Out shot a laser! Dr. Crisp carefully used it to draw an outline of a human heart in the air. Then she divided it into four parts.

"There! Each piece needs to go in one of those four spots. To move them, press this button," she said, showing them her watch. "Scan the piece you want to move, and then scan the spot you want to put it in. The Maker Maze will take care of the rest."

"I love when we get to use the lasers!" cheered Violet.

Dr. Crisp pulled a stethoscope out of her lab coat pocket and threw it over her head. As she caught it, she yelled, "Ready, set, SOLVE!"

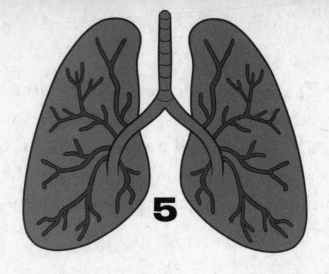

5

Violet, Pablo, and Lorenzo stood around the long lab table and examined the four different parts of Heather the Heart.

Violet put her hands on her hips and bit her lip. She glanced back at the floating outline. "I think these two go on the bottom," she said. She grabbed a blue piece and a red piece. "That's where it looks like they fit." She pointed.

"They kind of look like chili peppers," said Lorenzo.

"Yum!" Dr. Crisp pulled a small bottle

of hot sauce from her bag on the floor. "I like my science *spicy*." She pretended to shake it onto fake food.

"My mom keeps hot sauce in her purse, too." Pablo giggled.

"Well, your mom and I have something in common," said Dr. Crisp with a wink. "I never leave the lab without it! But then again . . . I never leave the lab."

The trio eyed Dr. Crisp.

"Never?" Lorenzo repeated.

Dr. Crisp shrugged, then said, "You Makers should get a move on!"
She held her watch in the air.

"We've already been here for twenty minutes! We have one hundred Maker Minutes left, and we haven't done anything," Pablo cried.

Violet shook her head. "Pablo, you worry so much that one day you're going to turn into a wart!"

"Ewwwww!" Lorenzo laughed and pointed at Pablo.

"Hey!" Pablo complained, scrunching his face.

"Just stand back," Violet continued. She fired the laser and scanned the piece.

"Okay, which side should the red one go on?"

"No idea," said Lorenzo.

"We just need to guess. Try the right side," Pablo said.

Violet aimed her watch at the lower right corner of the heart outline.

BIZZAP!

The red piece zipped from the table into the air and wiggled into the correct spot.

RING, DING, DONG!

"Yes!" cheered Lorenzo. "Can I do the next one?"

"Sure!" said Violet.

Lorenzo blasted his laser at the similarly shaped blue part. He sent it to the bottom left corner of the heart outline.

"Okay, the other two are easy. They must go on top," said Pablo. "Do you think red goes on top of red?" he asked.

"I'm not sure. Try!" said Violet.

Pablo used his watch to place the final two parts.

RING, DING, DONG!

"Phew," said Lorenzo. "This might be tougher than wrestling!"

Dr. Crisp squatted and flexed her muscles as she pretended to lift weights. "Science is a sport in the Maker Maze. You got this!"

"Okay, now we just have to figure out which way blood flows." Pablo held his chin between his thumb and pointer finger. "Blue blood comes into the heart," he began. "I mean, blood with less oxygen"—he paused to look at Violet—"so I bet blood enters the heart through here." He pointed to the blue side.

"That means that blood must enter the heart through the left side and leave the heart through the right side!" added Violet.

The room was silent.

"Did we get that right?" asked Lorenzo. He stuck a finger under his cast to scratch his arm.

"Nope," replied Pablo. "Violet forgot something. . . ."

Violet crossed her arms. "What do you mean?"

"We're *looking* at the heart," Pablo said. "If it was in our bodies, the blue side would be on the right."

"Ohhh, you're right," said Violet.

"You're going to need to learn more about the body if you want to cure diseases one day," Pablo teased.

"Hey! That's not funny," replied Violet.

Pablo held his thumb and pointer finger together and looked through them at Violet. "It was just a little joke." Then he

said, "Blood enters the heart on the *right* and is pumped out on the *left*!"

RING, DING, DONG!

"Blastin' blood vessels!" cheered Dr. Crisp. "You had *my* heart racing! But I knew you'd pull it off. Now let's race to level two!" She pulled the Maker Manual from her backpack. It flew open, and the

pages flipped until landing on one that
read:

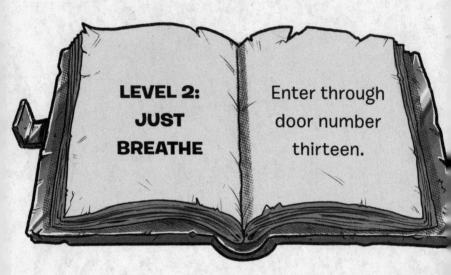

**LEVEL 2:
JUST
BREATHE**

Enter through
door number
thirteen.

Dr. Crisp closed the book and tossed it
back into her bag. Then she sprinted out
of room number eight and led the Makers
through the never-ending hallway to their
next stop.

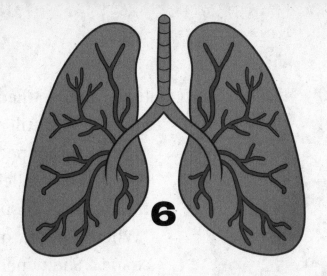

6

"There's nothing in here," said Lorenzo. His voice echoed off the bright white walls of the empty room.

Violet laughed. "Just wait. I'm sure Dr. Crisp has something fun up her sleeve."

Dr. Crisp shook out her arms. "Nope, nothing up there! But I do have something for you in here," she said with a wink. She opened her backpack and started to dig through it. "Watch out, Makers! Big bottle coming through!" she shouted. She

pulled and pulled and *pulled,* until a giant bottle popped out. It was taller than Dr. Crisp! "Whew, I'm out of shape." She wiped her forehead and continued digging. She pulled out a wide straw, a skinnier straw, tape, three large balloons, a clump of modeling clay, and a pair of scissors.

"Are we making another boat? Are we going on a cruise through the human body?" Violet asked.

"Yuck," said Lorenzo, grabbing his stomach. "I might have to sit this one out."

Dr. Crisp laughed. "No tummy cruises

today!" she said, rubbing her stomach. "You are going to make lungs!"

"Yes!" Pablo and Violet cheered.

Lorenzo tilted his head. "How are we going to do that?"

Dr. Crisp grabbed the Maker Manual out of her backpack and opened it. She removed a pencil from behind her ear and pointed it to a list of instructions. "Like this," she said with a smile. She passed the book to Lorenzo.

BIZZAP!

A shiver ran down Lorenzo's back. "Tingly!" he said.

Dr. Crisp took a deep breath—so deep her stomach ballooned past her lab coat! She finally let the air out and shouted, "Ready, set, MAKE!"

Violet and Pablo huddled around Lorenzo to read the instructions.

"First, we need to cut the bottom of the bottle off," said Pablo.

"I don't think these scissors are big enough." Lorenzo looked down at the small scissors on the floor, then up at the big bottle towering over the Makers.

"Not with those," responded Violet, pointing at the directions. "With this!" She held up her Magnificent Maker Watch. "Stand back!" Violet pressed a button on the side of her watch to launch her laser.

BIZZAP!

She aimed it at the bottom of the bottle and slowly circled it. The laser cut right through! "Timber!" she hollered as she gave the bottle a push.

CRASH!

The bottle tumbled over like a tree falling in the forest.

"That was . . . ," began Lorenzo, "AMAZ-ING! I love it here."

"A-MAZE-ment is our specialty!" cheered Dr. Crisp from the sideline. "And science, too, of course."

"Okay, let's cut the end off one of the balloons and stretch it around here," said Violet. She pointed to the open end of the bottle she had just cut. She turned to Lorenzo. "Can you help me?"

"I can help, too," said Pablo with a confused face.

"But I'm the biggest," Violet explained. "And Lorenzo is stronger than you. Even with only one arm." She giggled.

Lorenzo flexed his arm and smiled.

But Pablo frowned. "That's mean, Violet."

"It's not mean; it's true! And we need to hurry!" Violet showed him her watch. Eighty Maker Minutes left.

Pablo sighed.

"Why don't you cut the straws and tape them together?" suggested Lorenzo. "They're kind of long, but not heavy. You also need to stick the two balloons on the ends." Lorenzo pointed to a picture in the Maker Manual.

Pablo mumbled a reply under his breath and started working. He followed the directions and cut the long, skinny straw in half. He stuck the two halves inside the wider straw to make a Y shape. Then he added tape to fix them in place. Meanwhile, Violet and Lorenzo stretched the cut-open balloon over the bottom of the bottle.

"We need to blast a hole in the cap. Do you want to try, Lorenzo? It's super fun," said Violet.

"Sure!" he replied.

Lorenzo walked over to the top of the bottle and aimed his laser at the cap.

BIZZAP!

"Done!" he shouted.

"Okay, now we have to stick the straws . . ." Violet's voice trailed off. "Oh no! We went out of order!" she said, looking up at her friends. Violet's head fell back. She slammed her palm to her forehead. "First, we put the straws inside the bottle through the cap, with the two balloons facing down inside the bottle. *Then* we stretch the balloon over the bottom."

Dr. Crisp pulled two purple pompoms out of her lab coat pockets. "It's okay to make mistakes," she cheered.

"Magnificent Makers have what it takes!" She kicked one foot up to her hand and shook the pom-poms together.

Pablo folded his arms and tapped his foot. "Well, you two are big and strong. I'm sure you can fix it in no time."

Violet sighed. "Come on, Lorenzo." They struggled to remove the balloon. Eventually they got it off, and Pablo grabbed the Y-shaped straws with balloons attached. He walked inside the bottle and stuck the long end through the cap.

"There," he said, dusting his hands off. "Those must be the lungs." He gave one of the balloons a flick.

Violet and Lorenzo worked to reattach the balloon to the bottom of the bottle. When they finished, Pablo grabbed the modeling clay and sealed off the gaps between the straw and the hole in the cap. The friends worked together to stand the giant model lungs upright.

RING, DING, DONG!

"Flaming funnels! You all are on fire!" cheered Dr. Crisp.

"Yes!" Lorenzo celebrated with a victory dance. "What's the next level?"

"We're not done yet, champ! It's time to put these lungs to the test and figure out how we . . ." Dr. Crisp paused to take another deep breath. Her face turned redder and redder, until she finally released her breath and said, *"Breeeeeeathe!"*

Then she raised her arms and quickly lowered them while shouting, "Ready, set, THINK!"

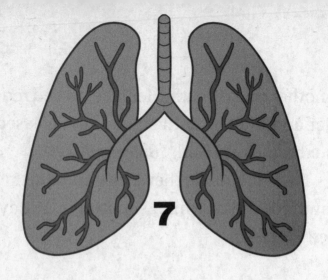

7

"Isn't the answer kind of easy?" Lorenzo shrugged. "We breathe by filling our lungs with air."

The room remained silent. No Maker Maze jingle.

"Yeah, but we need to figure out exactly how," Pablo explained. "Like, how the air gets into our lungs."

"I mean, don't we just suck it in?" said Violet.

"I think we should figure out how the

model lungs work," suggested Pablo. "That's why we built them."

Lorenzo thought for a moment. "I'm pretty sure the bottle is our body. The balloons must be the lungs. What about the straws?"

"What were those two hard words on our worksheet again?" asked Pablo, scratching his cheek.

"I think the two straws connected to the lungs are the *BRON-kye*," said Lorenzo. "I got bronchitis last year, and my doctor said it was because the tubes going into my lungs were swollen."

"*TRAY-kee-uh* was the other one," Violet remembered. "I bet the wide straw is the trachea. Mr. Eng said it connects our mouth to our lungs."

"So air comes into the body through

the trachea and gets to the lungs through the bronchi," said Lorenzo.

"But how? *That's* what we need to figure out!" Pablo groaned. He looked at his watch. Forty-five minutes left. There was time, but not much of it.

45 min. left

"So far this challenge hasn't been too hard," said Violet. "I bet the answer is super simple and we're just overthinking it." Then she paused and looked at the top of the bottle. "I have an idea. Can you both hold this steady for me? I want to climb up to the top."

"I don't think that's a good idea," said Pablo. "You could fall!"

"Relax, worrywart!" Lorenzo laughed.

Pablo's eyebrows scrunched together. The corners of his mouth became stiff.

"Pablo, we need to figure out how we breathe. And you just said we should use the model to solve the level," Violet insisted. "That's what I'm doing!"

"I know, but . . ." Pablo's voice trailed off as he gazed up at the giant model lungs. "It doesn't seem safe. Why do you want to climb up there anyway?"

"To blow into the straw. That should fill the lungs with air," Violet explained.

"But that's not even how we breathe!" Pablo replied. "I don't think lungs work like that."

"Well, you *did* think that blood was blue," mumbled Violet.

Lorenzo laughed. "Roses are red; blood isn't blue! Pablo's always scared; that's *definitely* true!"

Pablo felt a tingly feeling in his chest that crept up into his throat.

"Fine!" he shouted. "If you are going to be mean, then you both can figure this out on your own!" Pablo stomped off and sat in a corner of the room.

"Pablo! We're just messing around. We want to finish this challenge in time so

we can come back!" Violet hollered to her best friend.

But Pablo ignored her.

Violet's shoulders fell as she sighed. "I guess me and you have to finish on our own," she said to Lorenzo.

"Do you still want me to hold the bottle for you?" Lorenzo asked.

"Sure, thanks," Violet replied with a forced smile.

With Lorenzo holding the bottle on one side, Violet jumped up on the other. She hugged the bottle tightly with her long arms and legs. She started to shinny up.

"You're almost there!" shouted Lorenzo from below.

Violet climbed to right under the cap. She grabbed it with one hand and started to pull herself up. But she began to slip!

Violet dangled by one hand from the top of the model lungs.

"Help!" she shouted.

"I can't!" responded Lorenzo. "If I let go of the bottle, it will tip over! You'll crash to the ground!"

Pablo's eyes darted from the floor to his best friend. He stood up and shouted, "Violet! Be careful!"

But it was too late. Violet lost her grip and began falling toward the floor. Then suddenly, a voice boomed.

"MAKER MAZE, FREEZE!"

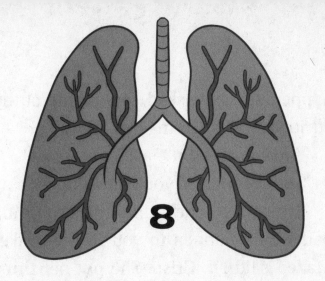

8

Violet's curls hung a few inches above the floor. She was frozen! Just like her friends back in Mr. Eng's class.

"Is she okay?" asked Lorenzo.

"She will be soon," responded Dr. Crisp. Then she shouted into her watch, "Maker Maze, unfreeze!"

Violet fell a few inches and landed on the floor with a thud.

"Ahhh!" she shouted, before realizing she was safely on the ground. "What happened?" she asked, looking up at the curious faces hovering over her.

"Are you all right?" asked Lorenzo.

"Dr. Crisp saved you!" said Pablo.

"I meant it when I promised nothing bad would happen to you in the Maker Maze," said Dr. Crisp. She put her three middle fingers down. "Maker's honor."

"That was scary," Violet said as she stood. Then she turned to her best friend. "I'm so sorry, Pablo. I really didn't mean to hurt your feelings. I promise. I was just trying to be funny," she said, looking down as she twiddled her fingers. Then she glanced up at Pablo and cracked a small smile. "But you know you can be a worrywart," she said softly.

Pablo smiled back. "I know. But it really felt like you were picking on me today. First because you beat me in our bike race. Then because I thought blood was blue. And it didn't help that you seemed to think Lorenzo was better than me at the challenge." He hung his head.

Violet didn't say anything. Instead, she gave Pablo a bear hug. "I'm sorry. Sometimes when I'm trying to be funny, I end up being mean. I'd never tease you on purpose."

"Are you okay?" Lorenzo asked Dr. Crisp. She was fanning her face and wiping away what looked like a tear from the corner of her eye.

"Well, flip my flask! You all are

making me teary-eyed," she replied, and cleared her throat. Then she knelt to look the Makers in the eye. "I think you learned a really important lesson today. We must be careful with the words we use. They can hurt. Even if we don't mean for them to."

"I'm really, really sorry," Violet said to Pablo. "I didn't realize I was hurting your feelings."

"Me either," added Lorenzo. "We're a team. And I'd never want to make a teammate feel bad. I'm sorry, Pablo."

"I know you didn't mean it. But sometimes a lot of little jokes add up. And turn into something not so funny." Then Pablo swung one arm around Violet's shoulders and the other around Lorenzo's. "But . . . I guess I do feel a little silly for thinking blood was blue."

The trio laughed.

"I hate to ruin the good vibes," Dr. Crisp interrupted, "but I think it's time to wrap up this level. Only twenty-five Maker Minutes left!" She held her watch in the air.

25 min. left

"This happens every time!" Violet moaned.

"It's okay," said Pablo. "I have an idea." He turned to Lorenzo. "Have you ever had the wind knocked out of you?"

"Yup! A bunch of times on the wrestling mat," he replied.

"When it happens, it's because someone hits you in the stomach, right?" asked Pablo.

"Yeah . . . why?" said Lorenzo.

"I think we breathe with our stomachs somehow," Pablo continued. "My mom does yoga all the time. The videos she watches always talk about breathing with your stomach."

"Oh yeah! And when Dr. Crisp took that big breath earlier, her stomach got huge!" Violet remembered.

"Can you two lift the bottle up a bit?" asked Pablo.

"No problem!" said Lorenzo, flexing his arm.

"I just need to get under it. That balloon is covering the cut-off bottle bottom for a reason," explained Pablo.

Violet and Lorenzo each stood on a side and grabbed the bottle. They lifted it high enough for Pablo to wiggle his way underneath.

"Okay, now look up and tell me what happens to the lungs!" he called from below. Then Pablo grabbed the rubber balloon and started to pull.

Violet and Lorenzo couldn't believe their eyes. The model lungs were working! Every time Pablo pulled on the balloon, the lungs would fill with air.

"Pablo, you did it!" cheered Violet.

"Yes! I knew it!" Pablo said as he wiggled back out from underneath the bottle. "It's our diaphragm!"

"Huh?" said Lorenzo.

"Our diaphragm. *DIE-a-fram*. I can't believe I forgot about it. I guess I didn't think of a muscle as being part of our respiratory system."

"Muscles help us breathe?" Lorenzo wondered aloud. "Cool!"

"That's right!" added Violet. "I can't believe I didn't think of it, either! My older cousin is a singer. She always talks about exercising her diaphragm so she can hold a note for a super long time."

Dr. Crisp cleared her throat and pretended to hit a high note. *"Mi mi mi mi miiiiiiii!"* she belted out.

"I think the bottom balloon is our diaphragm. That means when we breathe, it squeezes together. I bet that pulls air into our lungs. Like a vacuum! And *that's* how we breathe!"

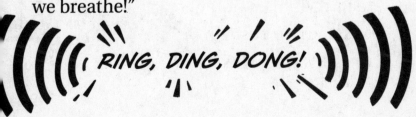

RING, DING, DONG!

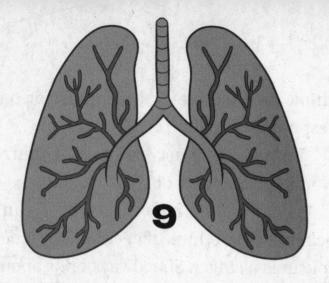

9

"**S**TEM-*tacular* work, Makers!" said Dr. Crisp. "I knew you all were going to figure it out!"

"How much time do we have left?" asked Lorenzo.

"Only twenty minutes!" cried Pablo. "We really need to hurry!"

Dr. Crisp rushed to pull the Maker

20 min. left

Manual out of her backpack. It flew open
to a page that read:

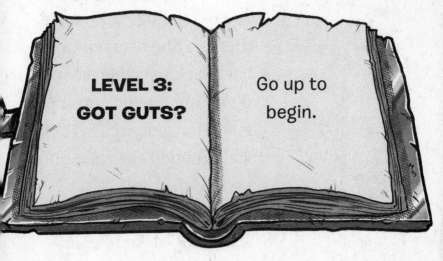

LEVEL 3:
GOT GUTS?

Go up to
begin.

"Up?" Violet asked as she bit her lip.
"Huh?"

Just then, a rope fell from a hole in the
ceiling. It swayed gently next to Dr. Crisp.

"Was that hole always there?" asked
Lorenzo.

Dr. Crisp didn't answer. Instead she

said, "I hope your lungs and muscles are strong! You're going to need them." She tossed her backpack over her shoulders and rolled up her lab coat sleeves. Then she grabbed the rope and started to climb.

"What about your arm, Lorenzo?" asked Pablo.

Lorenzo cracked his knuckles and smiled. "Watch this." He grabbed the rope with his unbroken arm. He squeezed the end of the rope between his legs. And he started to climb! He grunted his way to the top.

"Wow," said Pablo. His mouth dropped open. "He *is* strong."

"You are, too. Go for it!" Violet cheered on her best friend.

Pablo took the rope and began to climb. Violet followed.

∿

"Gross!" shouted Lorenzo.

"What are *those*!" said Violet, crawling through the hole.

"I'm sure that's what we have to figure out," Pablo said, catching his breath.

At the opposite end of the room, there were four floating holograms. One of them looked like a thin pink tube. The one next to it looked like a really big red jelly bean. The next two looked like sausage links. One was long and skinny. The other was shorter but wider.

Dr. Crisp spun on her heels to face the Makers and pressed a button on the side of her watch.

BIZZAP!

A laser shot out, and the names of four organs appeared in the air:

Stomach

Large Intestine

Small Intestine

Esophagus

Then Dr. Crisp clapped her hands. "Okay, Makers. Listen up! These are holograms of different organs in your digestive system." She pointed toward them with one hand. "And these are the names of each organ." Crossing her arms, she pointed to the list with her other hand. "To solve the level and complete the challenge, you must match the name of the organ with its hologram. Use your Magnificent

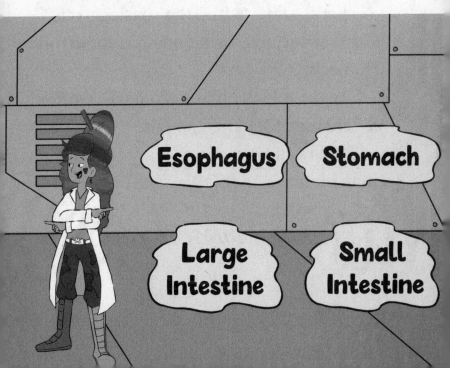

Maker Watches to scan each pair. And you better hurry. Only twelve minutes left!" She held her watch in the air. Then she raised her other arm and lowered them both rapidly. "Ready, set, MATCH!"

The Makers huddled to brainstorm.

"Let's start with the easiest one," Pablo suggested. "That one has to be the stomach."

"Yeah, it looks like a stomach. Go for it!" cheered Violet.

Pablo scanned the hologram and the matching word.

RING, DING, DONG!

"Those two holograms must be the intestines," said Lorenzo. "They look like . . . guts." He laughed.

"That means the long, skinny organ is the esophagus," Violet answered. "Remember what Mr. Eng said?"

"Yup," answered Lorenzo. "The esophagus sends food from your mouth to your stomach."

"I wonder if they call it a food pipe. Since the trachea is called a windpipe." Violet giggled.

The trio laughed.

"Scan it, Lorenzo!" said Pablo.

He aimed his watch.

RING, DING, DONG!

"Okay, just two—" began Pablo. But something caught his eye. He paused to look at Dr. Crisp, who was waving her arms in the air.

"Hate to burst your beaker, but time is almost up!" she cried, and pointed to her watch.

It was flashing purple.

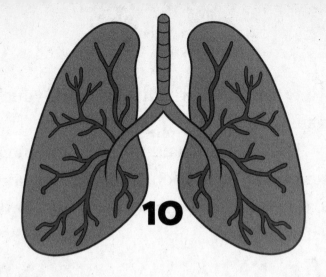

10

"**N**ot again!" Violet moaned.

"What does that mean?" asked Lorenzo.

Pablo grabbed his head with both hands. "It means we only have three minutes left!"

Violet took a deep breath. "We got this," she said. "We just have to figure out which is the large intestine and which is the small intestine."

"That one is longer," Pablo said, looking at the long, skinny intestine.

"But that one is wider," added Lorenzo.

"How can we tell which is large and which is small?"

"Let's just try," said Violet. She pointed her watch at the long, skinny one and scanned it. Then she scanned the words *Small Intestine.*

RING, DING, DONG!

"Yes! I got it right," she cheered. "Let's finish this!"

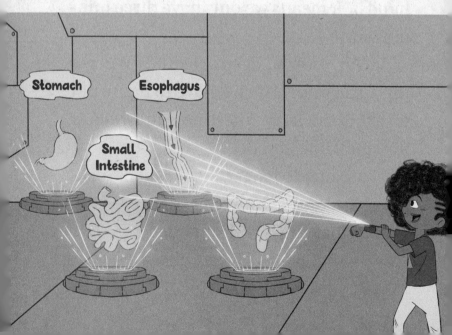

Pablo quickly aimed his watch and scanned the large intestine and the words to match.

RING, DING, DONG!

"Why is the small intestine longer than the large intestine? That doesn't make sense," said Lorenzo, studying the holograms.

"When it comes to intestines, *small* means skinny! Not short. Now, time to move!" shouted Dr. Crisp. "The portal is closing as we speak!" She darted over to the hole in the floor and flew down the rope to room number thirteen. One by one the Makers followed. They shot through the door and bolted as fast as they could down the long hallway.

By the time they made it to the main

lab, they could see the portal in the ceiling shrinking.

"We have to hurry!" shouted Pablo.

"How are we going to get through there?" asked Lorenzo.

"Jump!" Dr. Crisp yelled, running toward them. Just then, she slipped and fell to the floor! Her foot had slid on a dirty glove that she had thrown on the floor earlier.

"Are you okay?" asked Pablo with a worried voice.

"I'm fine. Just JUMP!" she hollered, pointing to the closing portal.

Violet, Pablo, and Lorenzo squatted and leaped as high as they could.

BIZZAP!

The trio rolled onto the floor of Mr. Eng's third-grade classroom. Everyone was still frozen.

"Hurry, let's get in our seats!" whispered Pablo.

Just as they sat down, everyone unfroze.

"Okay, class. Now let's . . . ," began Mr. Eng. But he paused when he noticed the model human body and all the organs tossed around on the floor. "What on earth happened here?" He shook his head and walked behind his desk to pick them up. "This was expensive! It shouldn't fall over so easily."

Violet, Pablo, and Lorenzo giggled.

Mr. Eng placed the model on his desk and put all the organs back in place. "There," he said, dusting his hands off on his pants. He continued with the lesson.

"Psssst!" whispered Lorenzo. He got Violet's and Pablo's attention and pointed to one of Mr. Eng's legs. He had a black smudge on his pants.

"Do you think we got him dirty when we came out of the portal?" Lorenzo asked.

"Maybe . . . ," said Pablo. "Hopefully he doesn't notice."

"Pardon me?" said Mr. Eng, looking at Violet, Pablo, and Lorenzo. "Did you have a question?"

The trio froze.

Then Violet smiled and said, "We were just thinking of an easier way to say *esophagus*. How does food pipe sound?"

Make your own creations!

⇒ MAKE MODEL LUNGS! ⇐

Always *make* carefully and with adult supervision!

MATERIALS

1 wide straw

2 narrow, bendy straws

3 balloons (don't blow them up!)*

   box cutter or small knife

   plastic bottle with a cap

   modeling clay

   scissors

   tape

You may want to have some spare balloons in case they rip!

INSTRUCTIONS

1. Cut the two narrow straws about an inch below the bendy neck and pull them to extend slightly. You will use the bendy ends and discard the other two pieces.

2. Stick the two ends of the narrow straws into the wide straw and use tape to secure them in place. They should fit very snugly and not be loose. It should look like a *Y*. This is your trachea!

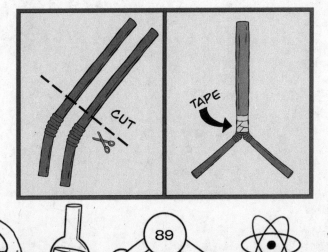

CUT

TAPE

3. Cut the neck off two of the balloons and use tape to attach each of them to one of the narrow straws. These are your lungs!

4. Use a box cutter or a small knife to *carefully* cut the bottom off the plastic bottle. Then use scissors to make a hole in the bottle cap. It should be just large enough to snugly insert the wide straw. Screw the cap onto the bottle.

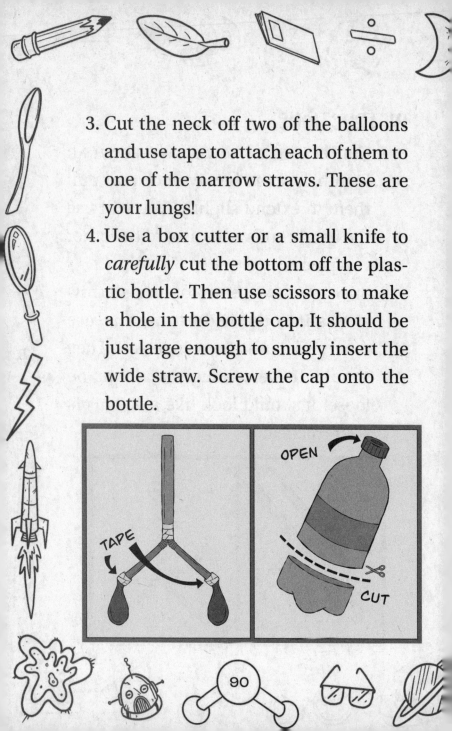

TAPE

OPEN

CUT

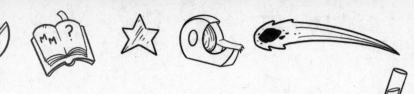

5. Insert the wide straw through the bottom of the cap. The two narrow straws and balloons should be below the cap inside the bottle. The wide straw should stick out of the top.

6. Use the modeling clay to seal off any gaps on top of the cap around the wide straw.

CLAY

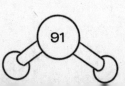

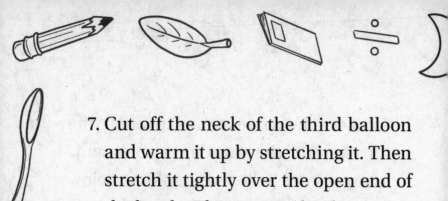

7. Cut off the neck of the third balloon and warm it up by stretching it. Then stretch it tightly over the open end of the bottle. That is your diaphragm!

8. Pull the bottom balloon and watch the lungs inflate!

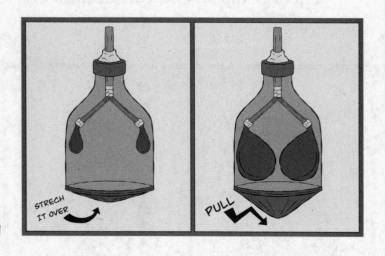

STRECH IT OVER

PULL

Your parent or guardian can share pictures and videos of your model lungs on social media using #MagnificentMakers.

92

≥ MAKE A MODEL HEART! ≤

MATERIALS

1 balloon (don't blow it up!)*

1 medium-sized plastic container (no lid)

1 toothpick or safety pin

2 bendy straws

2 small jars or drinking glasses

red food coloring

tape

water

You may want to have some spare balloons in case it rips!

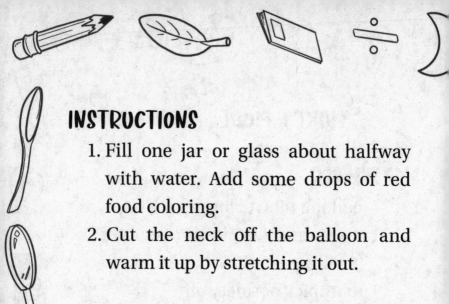

INSTRUCTIONS

1. Fill one jar or glass about halfway with water. Add some drops of red food coloring.

2. Cut the neck off the balloon and warm it up by stretching it out.

FOOD COLORING

CUT

3. Stretch the balloon tightly over the top of the jar or glass.

4. Take the toothpick or safety pin and poke one hole in the top of the balloon. Then poke a second hole about an inch away from the first. Try to make the hole as small as you can!

STRETCH IT

TWO HOLES

5. Push your straws through each hole. Make sure the bendy part is sticking out of the top.
6. Take the neck of the balloon that was cut off and use it to cover the end of one straw sticking out of the jar or glass.

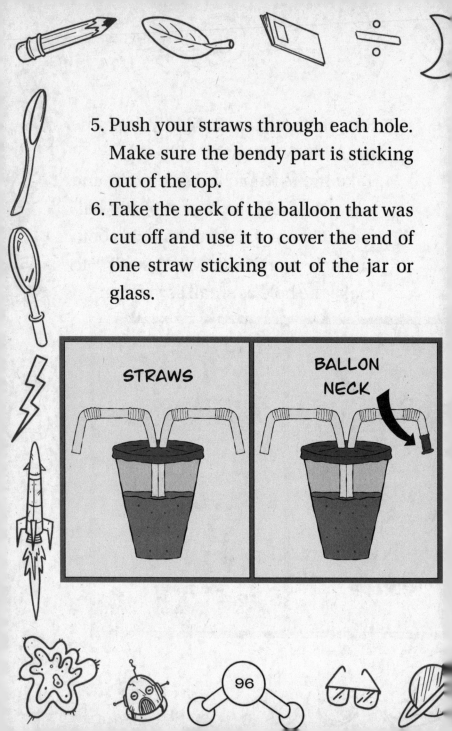

STRAWS

BALLON NECK

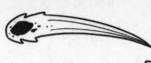

7. Set your jar or glass with straws in the plastic container. Place the other jar or glass underneath the straw that is not covered.

8. Start pumping! To pump, press your finger up and down on the stretched balloon and watch "blood" start to flow!

START TO FLOW

Your parent or guardian can share pictures and videos of your model heart on social media using #MagnificentMakers.

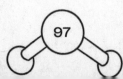

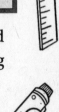

Missing the
Maker Maze already?

Read on for a peek at the Magnificent Makers' next adventure!

"**W**hew!" Violet wiped drops of sweat from her forehead. "Is it just me, or is it super hot today?" She grabbed her wild, curly hair and lifted it off her neck.

Pablo nodded and fanned himself with his hand. "I should've worn a T-shirt." He rolled up his sleeves.

The two best friends were on a field trip with their third-grade classmates from Newburg Elementary. It was Earth Day, and they were getting ready to tour the brand-new Environmental Science

Center. The students were excited to see what was inside. They had been waiting for a while already, and everyone was getting restless.

"Do you think actual scientists work here?" Violet asked Pablo.

"Probably," he replied. He scratched his cheek. "It is a science center after all. Hopefully we can go in soon and find out." He kept fanning his face.

Violet and Pablo became best friends in first grade when Pablo moved to Newburg from Puerto Rico. They had a lot in common and did just about everything together. They loved soccer and always played on the same team during recess. Their favorite color was red, and their favorite food was pickles. Especially the fried pickles they ate at the Newburg County Fair. They both also loved science.

Violet wanted to help people by becoming a scientist who studies different types of diseases. She was going to be the boss of her own laboratory one day. Pablo loved everything about space. He dreamed of becoming an astronaut and launching rockets when he grew up. Maybe he would be the first astronaut to meet an alien!

"Real scientists *do* work here!" their classmate Garry said. He was wearing a green shirt and standing behind Violet and Pablo.

The two best friends turned around.

"Really?" asked Violet, excited. "How do you know?"

"Well, my parents are two of the scientists who helped create this center," Garry replied.

"Your parents are *real* scientists!" Pablo exclaimed. His eyes grew wide.

"You're so lucky!" said Violet with her hands on her cheeks. "What kind of scientists are they? Do you have a lab in your house? Do you get to do experiments with them? Do they work here?" she asked, barely breathing between questions.

"I *wish* we had a lab at our house!" Garry giggled. Then he continued, "My parents don't work here. They work at the Newburg College. That's where their labs are. They study how to make solar panels better at turning light from the sun into electricity."

Pablo's eyes grew even wider. "*Whoa, that sounds hard.*"

Garry laughed again and shrugged.

Before Violet could ask more questions, Mr. Eng passed by with plastic water bottles in his hands. "They are almost ready for us," he said. "I brought these from the bus for you all." He handed one each to Violet and Pablo. They opened them and started gulping down the cool water.

"Here you go, Garry," said Mr. Eng with a bottle in his hand.

Garry smiled and shook his head. "No thanks. I don't like to use plastic."

"Are you sure?" Mr. Eng asked. "It's pretty hot out here."

"I'm sure," replied Garry.

"Okay then." Mr. Eng continued passing out bottles to the other students in line.

"What's wrong with plastic?" asked Pablo. "I thought it was okay to use as long as you recycle it."

Violet nodded with a mouth full of water.

"Recycling is good," said Garry. "But just like a trash dump, recycling plants produce pollution."

"Really?" asked Violet.

"Really," Garry repeated. "I have a reusable water bottle, but I forgot it at home today."

Violet looked at the plastic bottle in her hand and frowned. Just then, the doors to the Environmental Science Center opened.

"Welcome, students!" A woman with curly red hair and freckles smiled as she held the door open with her foot. "Sorry to keep you waiting. My name is Allie, and I will be your guide today. Come on in!"

Acknowledgments

Thank you for being an amazing partner, Jorge. You might be my biggest and most supportive fan. Mom, thank you for all the informal writing lessons. I learned from the best. I miss you. Dad, thank you for all that you have done for me and for all that you continue to do for our family. It's so wonderful having you close by now. The girls are lucky to have such an awesome Tata. To my beautiful daughters, Violeta and Lila, I love watching you grow and flourish. I can't wait to see how you change the world. So much of what I do is for you both. I hope I make you proud. To the entire Random House Team, Caroline Abbey, Tricia Lin, Lili Feinberg, Kimberly Small, and countless others, thank you! You all have been tremendously supportive, and I am privileged to be part of such an amazing and hardworking team. Finally, I'd like to thank my marvelous agent, Chelsea Eberly. I really mean it when I say you're the best. Thank you for your continued guidance and support!